THE OTHER SIDE OF THINGS

A SHORT STORY BY FELICIA GUY-LYNCH

Dedication

To all those striving
to maintain salvation

Praise for *The Other Side of Things*

"Wow! Where do I begin? A compelling and intriguing story, so relatable to real-life situations."
- Aziza Brown

"This short story has a worthy plot intertwined with nuggets of wisdom and wrapped in a tale of pain, struggle and hardship that many of us can connect with."
- Candace Shepherd

"Besides the sweet feeling of nostalgia, I like that the story touches on many issues teenagers are facing."
- Robert Mulolo

"Love it! The series is an enjoyable read, packed with life lessons and wisdom that can resonate with readers from all walks of life."
- Tessa Letang

"She does a great job of manifesting how the issues in the story are relevant to current events of today."
- Josephine Casey

"The *Finding Isaiah* Series served as a reminder to anyone that spirituality is not something to take for granted."
- Soul Szun

Preface

This book is the second short story to the *Finding Isaiah* series. The story will be told by the younger brother of the protagonist, Jafari. I chose to write from the insights of Isaiah's young brother because it will be interesting to see how he deals with life's challenges.

With all that said, I am pleased to present *The Other Side of Things* to you. It is hoped that your mind continues to be stimulated and accompanied by heightened anticipation.

Sincerely,

Felicia Guy-Lynch

Chapter 1

I guess it's my turn to tell you my side of things.

For starters, March break was cool until Isaiah got arrested the Friday before going to school. I miss him already.

I had to stay with Grandma until Mom came out. Staying with her wasn't all that bad. I loved cooking in the kitchen with her because it allowed us to bond. After burying Dad in May, Grandma sold Dad's shop and the Mississauga townhouse on Mom's behalf.

Our family has been through a lot lately but we did have good times. I'm holding onto them dearly.

I know it's beyond my reasoning but I just don't understand why Dad had to go out and disrespect Mom like that. I just wish he stayed true to her. He would probably still be alive today. Even though she's still in jail, I can always count on her.

Come to think of it, I knew something wasn't right about Susie (Dad's mistress). It just wasn't my place to say anything to him.

I remember Dad being upset with me for telling Isaiah about his mistress. I didn't care because although he was my father, I never felt like I had to keep any of his dirty secrets.

Deep down, part of me felt like he didn't want Isaiah to know because he knew how much Isaiah looked up to him. How long did he really think he was going to keep it a secret? Better yet, how long did he think it would take before Mom found out? She ended up finding out about Dad's infidelity after he got murdered.

When I moved to Brampton to stay with Grandma, I went to Bramalea Secondary School. That's when I met Carol. We took the Family Studies class together. I got to know her better when she was in my group to bake muffins. The muffins turned out nice but she was sweeter.

After 3 months of getting to know each other, she was my girlfriend.

Unlike Isaiah, I wasn't the brightest in school. It's not because I didn't understand what was expected of me. It's really because I couldn't connect with what the teachers were teaching us. I'm more of a hands-on learner, Mom called me, "Chef Jafari." Chef Boyardee got nothing on me. I loved the Food Network. My favorite show was *Emeril Live*.

In between cooking, I loved to go swimming. One thing I learned is in life, you sometimes have to go with the flow (especially with the things you don't see coming).

Like life, money should flow the same way. If that was the case, poverty wouldn't exist.

When things were better, I used to get Mom to drive me to the *Youth Without Shelter* to donate home-cooked food. No person my age deserves to go hungry. I wanted to be a part of the solution.

Unfortunately, Haze didn't stay on the right path. He started acting out. I knew he knew better. He probably got tired of doing good and being taken for a fool. I remember Isaiah telling me that Haze's father was very abusive towards him. It seems as though ever since Isaiah went to jail, Haze couldn't bear to fly solo. He started to hang out with the guys who weren't as cool as Isaiah. I hung around Haze because he offered to take me under his wing while Isaiah served time. Plus, school was soon coming to an end. He stopped taking lessons from Jeonsa because he felt like it wasn't the same. Although I wasn't fond of Martial Arts, I personally thought Haze was better off sticking to Tao Kwon Do.

"Why don't you practice Martial Arts anymore?" I asked Haze.

"Why you wanna know?" Haze asked.

"Because you seemed more focus when you were practising," I said.

"It's just not the same,"

"How so? Isn't changing for the better important?"

"Because I have to start wondering who my *real* friends are, changing for the better is important when it's necessary."

"Necessary for who?"

"Myself."

"When you say 'real friends,' are you referring to Isaiah?"

Haze replied, "Maybe. I don't know. I'm just sorting things out in my mind right now. Seeing how I can pick sense out of nonsense. Take what I hear with a grain of salt but it's easier said than done."

I pondered on what could possibly make him question Isaiah's integrity.

As I reminisce, I will never forget the weekend Dad got stabbed.

Grandma told me she found out from Mom that Winston (one of Dad's workers) turned himself in along with his two accomplices for orchestrating the robbery and attempted murder. Winston's guilty conscience must have really been killing him. I was shocked because everyone knew and loved Dad. He just wasn't the type of guy that would have a lot of enemies. But then again, if

Jesus had enemies doing nothing wrong. Who am I to think my Dad won't attract his enemies? Two weeks later, I found out Winston got murdered in prison.

The day Dad got stabbed, I remember being at the Scarborough Village Recreation Centre. My day was going so well and my swimming was only getting better. When Isaiah picked me up, I felt the energy in the car was too low. Subtly dreadful. The silence screamed mourning.

After Isaiah and Naomi broke the news, I knew things would never be the same. I didn't sleep well that night and broke down a couple of times.

Seeing Dad after being hospitalized was bitter-sweet. It was sweet because he was still alive but bitter because of what happened to him.

When Mom and Isaiah weren't home, I made sure Dad was ok. He loved when I cooked chicken roti and peanut punch mixed with malt. While eating around the table, I wanted to see where Dad's mind was at. "Dad. Who do you think did this to you?" He looked me in my eyes. Chewing slowly. Pondering. I waited in anticipation.

"I don't know. It could be anyone," he said.

"Everyone loves and respects you. I'm still shocked his happened to you."

"Yea. Well, I guess everyone has their arch-nemesis."

"What do you mean?"

"I mean, everyone has a foe. It's just more dangerous when you don't know who they are. Right now, I can't spend my time speculating and growing bitter. I just need to focus on getting better to go back to work,"

"That's true," I said.

An hour later, the police rang the doorbell. I answered and they told me they had a warrant out for Mom's arrest. She got charged with fraud. I was even more stunned.

They came in, handcuffed Mom, read her rights as she remained silent. The silence quickly turned into hysteria. She apologized so much that she started to sound like a broken record. I saw the shame and remorse in her eyes. They also seized her car. I had another sleepless night. I started to feel like our family was breaking down at an accelerated rate. It's like all these hard times came out of nowhere. Dad went straight to his room and slammed the door. I went to the community centre to go swim my tension off. I needed some sort of escape.

Not every boy grows into a man. Some think they're men but they are really just grown children with chin crumbs and hair at their front. A man keeps it real. He doesn't need to proclaim that he's the real deal because his aura exudes his transparency.

I find there are many fellows that want to get their shine on but don't really want to put in the work. I see the same old, same old but nothing original. A man is a trailblazer in his own right. He leaves the pathfinders for copycats to follow.

And then there are guys who act like they're the best thing since sliced bread. I know I got faults so I don't even act like I have it all figured out. I just focus on what I have to do and not focus too much on what other people are doing. I have no time for that.

Even though Isaiah is someone I always look up to, eventually, I need to grow into my own man. Besides

Dad, Isaiah was my hero. He was very popular. I'm not Tyrese but I was the *Baby Boy* of the bunch.

Like Dad, if Isaiah had haters, it was because they couldn't find any dirt on him. He was somewhat of a Goodie Two-Shoes. When times got rough, he seemed unaffected. Almost indifferent.

Surprisingly, I never really saw Isaiah with a lot of girls. Naomi was always the apple of his eye. Maybe he had a girl here and there but I never saw them. Whenever Naomi came around, I could tell Isaiah was smitten by her presence. Come to think of it, Naomi is kind of cute though. I know I'm too young for her and that she would never look my way. I'm cool with that.

Chapter 2

We moved to a townhouse in Mississauga Valley in February 2008. Valentine's Day, Isaiah and Naomi couldn't contain themselves. I found it annoying to have to wake up to my brother sexing his wife. The doorbell rang and it was like 3 o'clock in the morning. To me, that can't be anything good because they call it the Witch Hour. I got up to go tell Isaiah because I was not about to go downstairs by myself with no protection. I barged in only to find Naomi making love to my brother. Whoops.

"Isaiah?"

"Damn Jafari! You couldn't knock?" Naomi asked out of sexual frustration and embarrassment. "Damn it!"

"Don't do that again!" Isaiah exclaimed.

"Sorry guys but there's someone by the door," I said. "I think it's Haze."

"Ah, man. What does he want?" Isaiah asked. Irritated.

"Why don't you go downstairs and find out?" I suggested.

"Is everything ok?" Naomi asked concerned.

"Don't worry," Isaiah abruptly told Naomi.

"How long has he been there for?" Isaiah asked me.

"Not even a minute?" I said.

"Seriously. Baby. What's going on?" Naomi asked feeling uneasy.

"Don't worry about it I said," Isaiah demanded. "Stay here and don't go anywhere." Isaiah went to go take out his gun from the shoebox from underneath his bed.

Afterwards, he charged downstairs and I was right behind him. As soon as he got on the main floor, he took his time towards the front window. He slightly pulled back the curtain and looked outside. There was Haze. Standing and waiting while we didn't know what to expect. Isaiah finally opens the front door, concealing the gun behind his back.

"What do you want man?" Isaiah asked Haze.

"You're a dead man!" exclaims Haze.

After Haze threatened Isaiah, he simply walked away. Isaiah and I stayed up to keep an eye out. I grew more and more wary of their deteriorating relationship all because of some girl. Shame.

A week before that, I do recall the beginning of this deteriorating relationship. I was sitting on the bleachers while I watched Isaiah and Haze play basketball at the Mississauga Valley Community Centre. I finished swimming for the day and just had to wait on them to finish their game.

Haze stayed by the basketball net and passed Isaiah the ball whenever he took a shot. I found Haze to be more distant and aloof. He was usually running jokes and full of joy but he seemed troubled.

"You got the Jones in your Bones for Renee?" Haze asked. It seemed to have come out of nowhere.

"Not even. It's more like the other way around." Isaiah replied.

"Are you saying you hit that?"

"No way!"

"Stay away from my girl. I'm warning you."

"She's all over me! She danced up on me! I can't believe you, man! It was just a dance. Nothing more. Besides, why are you catching feelings over a female that you just met? You barely know her. Why are we even let-ting a female get in between our friendship right now?"

"Just stay away from my girl yo."

After seeing that, I knew things would never be the same between the two.

Chapter 3

July 2008 was a milestone. Mom was set to come in the middle of the month.

When Mom came out, she decided to stay with Grandma to regroup. Too many scars in Scarborough.

A week after Isaiah got released from jail, I got sent to the office for listening to music while he taught Shakespeare.

I waited 10 minutes before being able to speak to Principal Walters.

"Are you in or out?" he asked.

"In or out of what?"

"Are you in this to help me help you or do you want to call it quits?"

"I don't know."

"How are things at home?"

"It's whatever."

"Isaiah got out of jail last week."

"Yup. I know."

"I used to coach him on the basketball team. You know that. Right?"

"Yea."

"On the court, he was like Michael Jackson. Brilliant. Off the court? He's still a good guy. It's just that he got caught up trying to defend himself."

"What's that got to do with me?"

"Everything. I know how much you look up to him. And I'm sorry to hear about your father."

"Nothing can bring him back."

"I know you're dealing with a lot right now. To be frank, you shouldn't be in school considering the amount of classes you skip."

"I don't care."

"I need you to start caring. I'm fighting to keep you in school because I believe in you. I've arranged for you to complete your hours at the Terry Miller Recreation Centre every day after school. You will assist the Youth Workers for the after-school program."

"Why do you care so much?"

"Because you're worthy. You have 40 hours to complete. You have to complete 2 hours each day. 10 hours a week. You will be able to complete your hours by October. Miss a day without a good excuse and I will have to let you go. Do we have a deal?"

"Yea."

Chapter 4

Isaiah didn't want us to come visit him in jail. He didn't want to show his face. Only Naomi could come visit him. They ended up getting married while he was serving time. Also, his good behaviour granted him a reduced sentence. He got released 2 months later.

"Isaiah!" I said with excitement.

"Give me a hug man," he says while grabbing me. "How's school?"

"It's alright. You got big though."

"Bumping iron young fellow. You're still as skinny as you were from I last saw you."

"Man. Whatever. Check this out: my new tattoo."

"When did you get that?"

"July. Haze did it."

"Haze?"

"Yup."

"Man. I hope you been keeping out of trouble."

"My baby!" Mom said while smothering him.

After all the meeting and greeting, there was a knock at the door.

"Hey, Mom."

"Hey, Haze."

"I came to see Isaiah."

"Come on in."

Isaiah comes out from the bedroom, excited to see Haze.

"Dang. You got big!" Haze told Isaiah.

"Good seeing you man," said Isaiah.

"Grab your stuff and let's go."

"Alright. Just give me a sec. Lemme have a word with Jafari."

Isaiah called me into the bedroom.

"Jafari. Do you have to finish your community hours within a month?"

"How did you know?"

"Don't worry."

"Man. Walters such a snitch!"

"Walters isn't the problem. I need you to - "

"You guys ready?!" Haze shouted, interrupting.

"I want to come with you guys," I said.

"Naw. Don't you have homework to do?"

"Yea but why can't I just come with you guys?"

"I'll explain when I get back," Isaiah said. "Coming Haze."

"I'm not a little kid anymore Isaiah." He ignored me and walked away to get his jacket. What was he hiding?

Chapter 5

It didn't take long for Isaiah to make a name for himself. He opened up his barbershop and called it *Isaiah's Cut*. One day, he had a word for us.

"You all are young and Black. This system is designed to tear you down. For us to kill one another on top of them killing us. I'm saddened by what happened to Trayvon Martin, Kendrick Johnson and Michael Brown. The Prison Industrial Complex is designed to make money off of the backs of our brothers in jail and prison. Why do you think we make 80% of the incarcerated population? The judicial system is full of unjust laws. So, I urge you: put faith in yourself. Not the system. They look at us as less than human since they enslaved us. And even though we're "free," we still gotta undo them mental chains. Like yo, we were more unified during the Civil Rights movement and The Black Wall Street. Integration destroyed that. The illusion of inclusion. No, I don't have all the answers but I do know in order to do the best for yourself, you gotta know yourself. Love yourself. We were once Kings and Queens. Trailblazers of Civilization. Let's stop pathfinding."

After Isaiah and Haze left, I completed my homework, washed the dishes and played some *Call of Duty on my* PS3. The door knocked and Mom went to go see who it was.

"Who are these two knuckleheads by my door?" she asked. "The door is for you Jafari."

I got up to open the door and it was the Bolsen twins from my math class. They came by to pick me up for the party. It was the same party Isaiah told me not to go to. I didn't care. I went anyways.

Chapter 6

I arrive at the party and it was live.

"Isaiah!" Naomi exclaimed. They embraced. I spotted them but they didn't see me. After kissing and hugging, they left. Within 5 minutes, Naomi is yelling at Isaiah. I went to go see what all the commotion was about.

"Why would you want to leave?! You're the King of the block!" It sounded like she was coming from a strange place of frustration and admiration.

"I don't want to be here anymore! I need a fresh start. I want to rebuild with you but I have business that needs to be taken care of. You said you would wait on me but you have a problem leaving. I don't get it," said Isaiah.

"Baby. We got you. You don't have to go anywhere."

"No. I'm not settling. You shouldn't either. Let me take care of you."

"I'm not going anywhere!"

"Never mind."

"Never mind what?"

"Come with me or get left behind."

"Who the hell are you?! Where is Isaiah? I want my husband back!"

"He's right here in front of you! You just can't see."

"What's going on man? Everything ok?" Haze asked Isaiah.

"Not even," Isaiah replied.

"Chill out," Haze told Isaiah. "Since you've been gone, we've been expanding our territory. Now that you're back, you can help with that. We've been missing you out here."

"I was never into all that. Don't try to initiate me."

"You just need more time to think about it."

"I've done enough thinking."

"Go chill. Cool off then we can talk."

"It doesn't matter. You're corrupting the youth."

"Corrupting?"

"You're a coward. I did 6 months in jail. I'm not going back and I'm not letting you drag Jafari into this!"

"Remember who you are talking to."

"I know who I am talking to. I'm out of here. Jafari is done too. Touch my family and you'll another side of me you're going to regret I came out."

"Jafari's a soldier. He needs me to guide him and that's what I'm going to keep doing."

"Come near my brother again and I'll come to your funeral to make sure your Mom is reading your eulogy."

"I don't need to come to Jafari! He comes to me!"

Isaiah knocked Haze out cold.

"Isaiah!" screamed Naomi.

"Leave me alone!"

"Where are you going?!"

Isaiah ignored Naomi and started looking around until he spotted me.

"Let's go!" he told me.

"Why are you like this?" I asked him.

"I didn't want you to see this. That's why I told you to stay home with Mom."

"That's messed up."

"You're not going back."

"Says who?"

"Me!"

"Why are you acting so different? What happened?"

"Being in jail tore me up because I couldn't be there for you. I have to move different now."

I might have a change of heart.

Isaiah got ready to go check in with his parole officer and walked me to school the next morning. We went to Tim Horton's. He bought me a twelve-grain bagel toasted with buttered and a large hot chocolate. After eating, he urged me to go home right after completing my community hours. I told him not to worry. He told me to keep my head up. That would be the last time I ever saw him.

School came and went. I was excited. I had two hours left to finish for my community hours. Just as I enter the building, shots rang. Boom. Bang. I got hit three times. Isaiah came flying out of nowhere. Weeping. Pleading. Holding me. Begging me to hang in there. I let go.